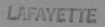

MARDI GRAS!

by Suzanne M. Coil • photographs by Mitchel Osborne

Macmillan Publishing Company • New York

Maxwell Macmillan Canada • Toronto

Maxwell Macmillan International • New York Oxford Singapore Sydney

For Jesse, René, Astrid, Christopher, and
all *the children of Louisiana, young and old*
—S.M.C.

For Jean, Lisa, and the krewes of
Comus, Momus, and Proteus,
who have given us so much
—M.O.

Text copyright © 1994 by Suzanne M. Coil. Photographs copyright © 1994 by Mitchel Osborne.
Macmillan Publishing Company is part of the Maxwell Communication Group of Companies. Macmillan Publishing Company, 866 Third Avenue, New York, NY 10022. Maxwell Macmillan Canada, Inc., 1200 Eglinton Avenue East, Suite 200, Don Mills, Ontario M3C 3N1. First edition. Printed in the United States of America.

10   9   8   7   6   5   4   3   2   1   The text of this book is set in 13 point Goudy Old Style. Book design by Constance Ftera.

Library of Congress Cataloging-in-Publication Data
Coil, Suzanne M.
Mardi Gras! / by Suzanne M. Coil ; photographs by Mitchel Osborne. — 1st ed.
p.   cm.
Includes index.
Summary: Examines the history and events connected with the annual pre-Lenten celebration in
New Orleans, such as the parades, balls, krewes, and the Acadian "Courir de Mardi Gras."
ISBN 0-02-722805-3
1. Carnival—Louisiana—New Orleans—Juvenile literature.   2. New Orleans (La.)—Social life and
customs—Juvenile literature. [1. Mardi Gras.   2. New Orleans (La.)—Social life and customs.]   I. Title.
GT4211.N4C65   1994   394.2′5—dc20   92-21166

Contents

Let's Go to the Mardi Gras!

It's marvelous, magical, mirthful, magnificent. It's Mardi Gras—the most fabulous party on earth—and *you* are invited.

Soon after Christmas each year, the people of southern Louisiana begin their celebration of Carnival, an exuberant explosion of parades and parties that reaches its grand climax on Mardi Gras. The most famous celebration takes place in and around New Orleans where costumed revelers take to the streets in a joyful riot of color and sound.

Many people think that Mardi Gras is just another name for Carnival, but the terms have different meanings. Mardi Gras, French for "Fat Tuesday," refers to only one day—Shrove Tuesday. Carnival, on the other hand, refers to the entire period from Twelfth Night (January 6) until midnight on Mardi Gras.

The day after Mardi Gras, Ash Wednesday, marks the beginning of Lent, the season of penance and fasting in the Christian religious calendar that ends on Easter Sunday. But Easter doesn't always fall on the same date; it can be as early as March 23 or as late as April 25. Because Mardi Gras comes exactly forty-six days before Easter, it can fall on any Tuesday from February 3 to March 9. That's why Carnival, which begins on January 6 and ends on Mardi Gras, can last only four weeks in some years and as long as eight weeks in others. However long it lasts, Carnival is always welcome.

Carnival is not just something to watch, it's something to be part of. It's a time for children and grown-ups alike; a time when an entire family can dress up like unicorns and not stand out in a crowd. It's a time for people of all ages, races, and religions to come together in a spirit of goodwill.

In a short while, it will all be over. So join the fun. As people in New Orleans say, "Let's go to the Mardi Gras!"

Mardi Gras: How Did It All Begin?

When people celebrate Mardi Gras, they are carrying on a tradition that dates back to ancient times, when spring festivals were held to ensure the fertility of animals and crops. These old festivals live on in Europe today and go by many names; *Fasching* in Germany, *Carnivale* in Italy, and *Mardi Gras* in France.

Mardi Gras came to America when some hardy French explorers landed near the mouth of the Mississippi River one day in 1699. Their leader, Pierre le Moyne, Sieur d'Iberville, noticed that it was March 3. Back home, people were celebrating Mardi Gras, so he named the spot Pointe du Mardi Gras in honor of the day.

Nineteen years later, his brother, Jean Baptiste le Moyne, Sieur de Bienville, founded a town along the river and named it Nouvelle Orléans. Before long, New Orleans became famous as a place where people knew how to enjoy themselves.

By the time Spain took possession of Louisiana in 1766, Mardi Gras was an established tradition. But the Spanish, who were straight-laced, banned the custom of wearing masks on the street, and Mardi Gras was driven indoors where it was celebrated privately by the Creoles (the descendants of early French and Spanish settlers).

In 1803, two years after taking it back from Spain, France sold Louisiana to the United States. Suddenly, droves of Americans descended on New Orleans. The Creoles didn't like the newcomers, whose language and manners were different from their own. The Americans, on the other hand, didn't approve of the French-speaking Creoles and their customs. They tried to suppress Mardi Gras, but the Creoles persisted and, in 1838, organized the first real street parade. In the end, Mardi Gras worked its magic on the newcomers.

In 1857, six young Americans formed a Carnival club called the Mistick Krewe of Comus, after Comus, the Roman god of revelry. They paraded on Mardi Gras night with two small floats followed by African-American servants carrying *flambeaux* (lighted torches), and costumed maskers on foot. New Orleans, which had never seen anything so magical, was delighted.

Comus, the oldest, most secretive Carnival organization, invented the word "krewe," and set the pattern of choosing a krewe name from mythology. With its parade of thematic floats, a private ball, mock royalty, and secret membership, Comus gave a form to Mardi Gras that has endured ever since.

The Krewes of New Orleans

The success of Comus inspired other people to form krewes. Before long, the Twelfth Night Revelers, Rex, Momus, and Proteus were born. Today, there are more than one hundred krewes.

In New Orleans, these private, nonprofit social clubs sponsor the immense parades that have made Carnival in the Crescent City world famous. They also hold dances and balls.

Every year, each krewe chooses a King and Queen to preside over its activities. Being chosen is considered a great honor. Even though it means wearing tights in public, there is hardly a man in New Orleans who would turn down the chance to be king. And, of course, all young girls dream of becoming a queen.

The real power in a krewe, however, is held not by the monarchs, but by the captain, whose identity is almost always secret. The captain's job is demanding. He oversees every detail of the krewe's activities, from the choosing of monarchs to the organizing of the parade.

Some of the famous krewes:

Rex ("king" in Latin) is the most famous krewe of all. Rex is also the name given to the king of the krewe. He is also King of Carnival, monarch to all the people, and he and his queen reign over Mardi Gras.

The krewe of *Bacchus*, named after the Greek god of wine, is famous for its innovative parades featuring animated floats, and for choosing famous people to play the role of Bacchus. Kirk Douglas, Bob Hope, Charlton Heston, Dennis Quaid, and Dom DeLuise are among the celebrities who have played Bacchus in years past.

Rex himself.   *A Bacchus float.*

The krewe of *Endymion*, named for the Greek god of eternal youth, has over 1,500 members, making it the largest krewe in Mardi Gras history. With thirty-five super floats, thirty-six bands, and more than five thousand participants, Endymion stages the largest, most exciting parade in the world.

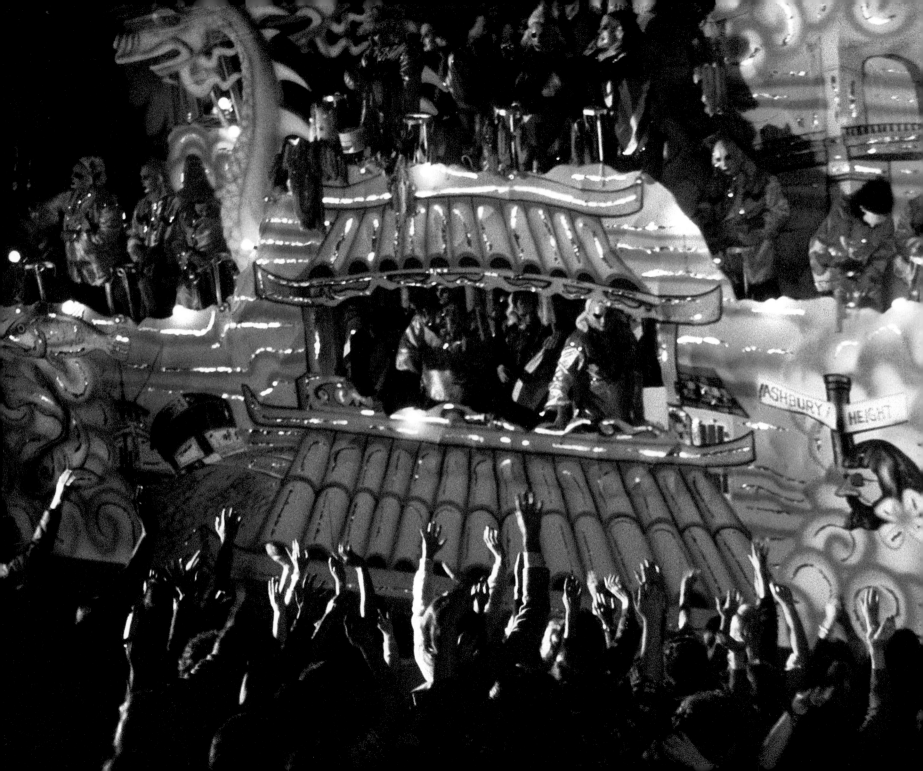

Zulu, the oldest African-American krewe, was founded in 1909. The first king of Zulu mocked the white "society" krewes, which would not admit African Americans, by carrying a banana stalk instead of a scepter and wearing a lard can as a crown. The most famous Zulu King was Louis Armstrong who reigned in 1949. Fortunately, Zulu has never lost his sense of humor and his parade on Mardi Gras morning remains one of the grand highlights of Carnival.

But the krewes are not the only organizations involved with Mardi Gras....

The Mardi Gras Indians

"Oooh! Here come the Indians!" someone shouts, as a thrill runs through the crowd. With plumed headdresses that can tower more than four feet high and robes covered with feathers, rhinestones, ribbons, intricate beading, and sequins, the Mardi Gras Indians are indeed a fabulous sight.

Every Mardi Gras, "tribes" with such names as the Wild Magnolias, the Golden Eagles, the Yellow Pocahontas, and the White Eagles, parade through their neighborhoods dancing to hypnotic music and hand-clapping rhythms. Although their past is shrouded in mystery, it is known that African-American Creoles (people of mixed African, American Indian, and French or Spanish descent) have preserved this tradition for more than one hundred years.

No one is certain how many tribes exist. Fewer than ten tribes actually parade, but excitement runs high wherever the Indians appear. Their processions often stretch ten blocks in length, and a tribe may march as many as thirty miles on Mardi Gras. As they pass through the streets, throngs of onlookers fall in to dance in the "second line."

Since the tribes have no set routes, whether or not they meet is a matter of chance. Years ago, their encounters often resulted in violence. Today, their "battles" are acted out in a thrilling ritualized dance that reflects both African and American Indian elements.

Because they never wear the same costume for more than one Mardi Gras, Indians spend months—sometimes an entire year—designing and sewing their new outfits by hand. The costumes are beaded with geometrical designs or with pictures of animals, birds, flowers, and Indian heroes. Thousands of beads, rhinestones, and sequins, as well as pounds of feathers, go into the making of each costume. With ostrich plumes costing more than two hundred dollars per pound, and rhinestones as much as seven dollars a gross (144), a

single costume may cost as much as five thousand dollars. Since most Indians are working-class people, their costumes represent an enormous financial burden. But their unique cultural heritage is a source of great pride to the Indians, and well worth the sacrifice.

Anyone lucky enough to witness the Mardi Gras Indians will never forget their great dignity and majestic splendor.

Parties and Balls

Carnival begins with parties and masked balls, and it ends the same way. They range from exclusive by-invitation-only masked balls—at which the season's debutantes are presented to society—to casual, private parties for families and friends.

For socialites, Carnival opens with the Twelfth Night Revelers Ball, when a lucky debutante becomes the first Queen of Carnival. Most masked balls feature a tableau in which costumed krewe members enact scenes based on history, literature, or legend. For example, guests at a recent ball were entertained by costumed krewe members who acted out a tale from the *Arabian Nights*. The tableau is followed by dancing and champagne.

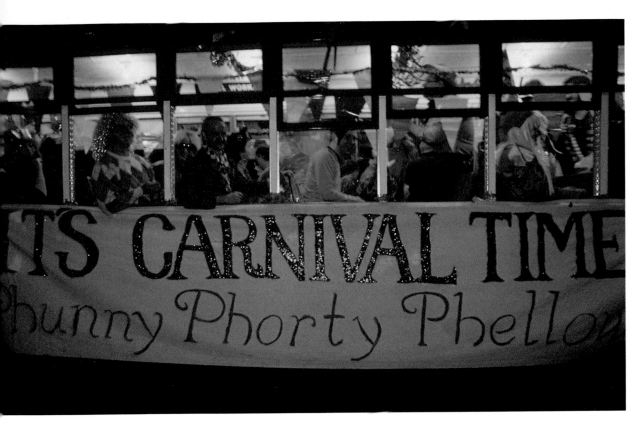

For those not invited to the Twelfth Night Revelers Ball (and that includes nearly everyone), Carnival is launched when the Phunny Phorty Phellows hold their annual Twelfth Night streetcar party. When these marvelous messengers of Mardi Gras ride through the city, the public knows that Carnival has arrived—and that it's time for king cake parties.

King cakes are oval confections decorated with carnival colors. Each cake contains a small baby doll to symbolize the finding of baby Jesus by the Magi. Whoever finds the baby must host the next party. King cake parties are so popular that more than 500,000 king cakes are consumed every year in the New Orleans area.

Although New Orleanians love parties, they love parades even more.

Parades, Parades, and More Parades

Beginning several weeks before Mardi Gras, nearly seventy large parades, each staged by a different krewe, take place around New Orleans. The parades feature large, elaborate tractor-drawn floats—neon-lighted floats, animated floats, and "super floats" that can tower two stories high—making Carnival in New Orleans the world-famous spectacle it is today.

Every parade is built around a theme, and each float depicts an aspect of that theme. In 1992, for example, Endymion's parade was titled "The World's Greatest Mysteries," and more than 1,300 krewe members rode on twenty-seven super floats illustrating such subjects as the Loch Ness Monster and "Secrets of Stonehenge."

Most Carnival parades follow the same pattern. The krewe captain leads the procession, followed by the krewe's officers, the king or queen, and in some parades, the maids and dukes. Next comes a

float announcing the parade theme, followed by floats bearing costumed krewe members. Between the floats are marching bands, dancers, clowns, and motorcycle units, so that a twenty-float procession may actually feature more than one hundred units and involve more than three thousand people. The largest parades may have as many as five thousand participants.

Every parade is the result of a great deal of work by an army of people. As soon as Mardi Gras is over, krewe members make plans for next year's parades. They choose a theme and call in artists to make detailed drawings of new floats and costumes. Once the drawings are approved, the work begins. And there's no time to waste. It can take a full year to complete a float. After a chassis is built, craftsmen construct a skeleton of wood, metal, Fiberglas, and other materials, over which giant papier-mâché figures and decorations are attached. The work is done in massive warehouses called "dens."

Every parade starts at a designated time and proceeds along an established route. On the day of their parade, krewe members gather in their den to don their costumes. Finally the doors are flung open, the floats emerge, and the parade begins.

There's only one problem in this parade lover's paradise—no one can get to see them all.

"Throw Me Something, Mister!"

In most places, people stand calmly on the sidelines, chatting with one another as they enjoy the passing parade. But not in New Orleans. There, float riders are greeted by roaring crowds shouting "Throw me something, mister!" "Pair of beads!" or simply "Hey! Hey!" Everyone is screaming for souvenir "throws." Maskers on the floats respond by flinging beads and other trinkets into the sea of upstretched hands while the crowd grabs and scrambles to catch the trinkets raining down on it.

By the time Mardi Gras is over, the average paradegoer will have hundreds of strings of cheap beads and a rich assortment of trinkets, everything from Frisbees and stuffed animals to bikini underwear and giant toothbrushes. Lucky paradegoers will catch Mardi Gras collectors cards, plastic cups decorated with krewe emblems, and an assortment of doubloons. Popular with collectors, doubloons are beautifully designed aluminum souvenir coins. The most fortunate paradegoer, however, will take home the rarest and most coveted throw of all: a decorated coconut, symbol of Zulu.

Who Pays for Carnival?

Carnival has been called "the greatest free show on earth." But the beautiful floats, costumes, and throws cost a great deal. Who pays for everything? The participants do. The governments of New Orleans and surrounding communities issue parade permits, coordinate parade routes, provide police and sanitation services, but they do not contribute any funding. By tradition and law, there is no official Mardi Gras sponsor. Commercial and political advertising are banned, and there's no such thing as an "authorized" Mardi Gras logo. Mardi Gras belongs to *everyone*.

The pleasure of participating in Carnival costs krewe members nearly $35 million every year. They spend $18.6 million on throws alone. Each of the 850 members of Bacchus, for example, pays $750 for membership dues and spends up to $1,500 on trinkets to throw to the crowd during its parade. Why would anyone spend all that money to hide behind a mask, and give things to people they've never met? Float riders have no trouble explaining their generosity. "Because it's Mardi Gras," they say. Or, as one rider put it, "You feel as though you're doing something good when you look into a crowd and see their happy faces and feel their wonderful mood."

Costumes and Masks

If you've ever dressed up on Halloween, you know how much fun wearing a mask and costume can be. You can pretend to be someone different and live a fantasy for a day; instead of watching the show, you become part of it. And when you're in costume, people are friendlier to you. That's why people who dress up on Mardi Gras have more fun than people who don't.

During Carnival, it's not unusual to meet tigers, pirates, princesses, Michael Jacksons, Ninja Turtles, and other fanciful creatures walking down the street. Costumes can be purchased and rented, but many people prefer to make their own, often spending months designing and sewing their elegant creations.

If you decide to dress up on Mardi Gras, let your creativity run wild. But remember, you'll have more fun if you wear something comfortable, unlike the inventive but confining costume worn by this reveler.

The Rhythms of Carnival

New Orleans is famous as the birthplace of jazz. No wonder, then, that the air is filled with music during Carnival.

Musicians are busy during Carnival. Bands are essential at balls and dances. And marching bands, which give the throbbing pulse to Carnival parades, are in high demand. A single parade can include many bands—Bacchus, for example, has used as many as sixty bands in its parade.

Marching clubs, such as Pete Fountain's Half Fast Walking Club, add a joyous note to Mardi Gras. To the infectious sounds of jazz classics like "When the Saints Go Marching In," they parade through the streets waving their flowered canes and trading flowers and fun for kisses.

Whenever the Mardi Gras Indians appear, their irresistible music sets people dancing. Accompanied by banging drums and tambourines, they sing intricate call-and-response chants, a tradition shared by both Africans and Native Americans. Some scholars say that their strong African-Indian rhythms inspired the music now known as New Orleans rhythm and blues.

The most popular rhythm and blues Carnival song is "Go to the Mardi Gras," written by the legendary Professor Longhair. But the most famous Carnival song is neither jazz nor rhythm and blues. It is, instead, a foolish song that has been the official Mardi Gras anthem for more than one hundred years.

If ever I cease to love,
If ever I cease to love,
May the fish get legs and the cows lay eggs—
If ever I cease to love!

How did such a silly song become the sound of Carnival? Like Mardi Gras itself, the story behind it is a royal fantasy of kings and queens and love.

"If Ever I Cease to Love"

Mardi Gras might not have some of its most cherished traditions were it not for a handsome twenty-two-year-old Russian grand duke, nephew of the tsar. The year was 1872 and His Imperial

Highness Alexis Alexandrovich Romanov had been invited to America to hunt buffalo. He stopped first in New York where he met a beautiful actress named Lydia Thompson. When Lydia sang "If Ever I Cease to Love," Alexis's heart melted. Then it was time to head west, but wherever he went, he couldn't forget Lydia. So when Alexis learned that she was going to New Orleans, he decided to go there, too.

Everyone in New Orleans was preparing for Mardi Gras. When news came that a genuine grand duke was about to arrive, the citizens decided to plan something spectacular. Mardi Gras was declared an official holiday. A new krewe—Rex—was formed and a King of Carnival was appointed to welcome the grand duke. Special Carnival colors were hurriedly selected: purple (for justice), green (for faith), and gold (for power). A reviewing stand was erected, complete with a throne, so that Alexis might enjoy the parade in comfort.

Finally, the grand duke arrived and that evening, at the Opera House, he saw Lydia again. On the following day, Mardi Gras, he marched up the steps of city hall, but declined to sit on the throne. After all, he explained politely, wasn't this a democratic country in which all men were created equal, and in which no special reverence was paid to royalty?

Alexis stood stiffly throughout Rex's first parade. And what a parade it was. Composed of carriages, wagons, and marchers on foot, the parade had more than ten thousand participants and stretched over a mile in length. Since everyone knew how much Alexis liked "If Ever I Cease to Love," band after band played the song. Before long, everyone was singing.

No one could tell what Alexis was thinking, but by the time Rex, the first King of Carnival, rode up on his horse to salute the grand duke, Alexis was stony-faced. He had an engagement with Lydia, but he broke it and never saw her again. A few days later, he left, leaving behind traditions that Mardi Gras has followed ever since: Rex as King of Carnival, an official holiday, and "If Ever I Cease to Love" as its song.

Courir de Mardi Gras

While the fabulous parades roll through New Orleans, the Cajuns of rural southern Louisiana celebrate a tradition that dates back to medieval times. It's called the *Courir de Mardi Gras*—the Mardi Gras Run—and it begins at dawn when groups of men and horses gather in the misty cold. All are dressed in outlandish costumes. Many wear masks made of painted wire screen and tall, cone-shaped hats. In fourteenth-century France, where the Courir tradition began, the costumes were meant to poke fun at aristocrats and the pointed hats ridiculed bishops.

When all are ready, the riders set off accompanied by wagons and pickups carrying musicians, refreshments, and those too timid to ride horses. Throughout the day, the riders race across the prairie, stopping at farms and homes along the way, where they sing and carouse in exchange for chickens and sausage.

The wild ride ends in late afternoon when the tired, bedraggled riders straggle into town. The chickens and sausages are added to the gumbo bubbling in a huge iron pot. Later, the whole town shares the gumbo, the last feast before Lent begins. After supper, the children are put to bed, and the party begins. The musicians play nonstop while the grown-ups dance the two-step and "pass a good time" until midnight comes, and with it, the end of another strange and wonderful Cajun Mardi Gras.

The Day After

It's late on Mardi Gras evening. Slowly, police move through the crowds announcing that when the clock strikes twelve, Carnival will be over and the streets must be cleared. As the revelers straggle off reluctantly, midnight comes, ushering in Ash Wednesday and the Lenten season of penitence and fasting.

Throughout the night, sanitation trucks rumble through the city picking up mountains of debris, and water-spraying sweepers wash down the streets. Anyone still outside must run for cover, or risk getting a cold shower.

Daybreak finds the streets strangely silent as tourists head for the airport, staggering under loads of bags filled with useless trinkets, wondering how they can ever explain the miracle of Mardi Gras to their families and friends back home.

Everyone is tired. But even as the city breathes a sigh of exhaustion, the spirit of Mardi Gras lingers in the air. People begin to dream of next year and the good times they'll have when Carnival returns.

In other places, suspending the rules often brings out the worst in people. But not in New Orleans. Although more than a million people come together to celebrate Carnival, there are few incidents to disturb the peace. That's because, with an instinct bred into their unique culture, the people of southern Louisiana share their courteous, generous spirit with everyone at Carnival. Just as throwing beads and trinkets reminds us that we all have gifts for one another, the spirit of Mardi Gras shows how people of different races, religions, and backgrounds can get along together.

So, come on down and "pass a good time."
Share the spirit. Join the fun.
Let's go to the Mardi Gras!

Index

Bold page numbers indicate where definitions may be found.